P9-DMU-341

Amelia Bedelia
Digs In

#12

Amelia Bedelia

Digs In

me

by Herman Parish

pictures by Lynne Avril

Greenwillow Books

An Imprint of HarperCollins Publishers

Gouache and black pencil were used to prepare the black-and-white art.
 Printed in the United States of America. For information address HarperCollins Children's Books, a division of HarperCollins Publishers, 195 Broadway, New York, NY 10007.
www.harpercollinschildrens.com

Library of Congress Cataloging-in-Publication Data is available.

ISBN 978-0-06-265843-2 (hardback)—ISBN 978-0-06-265842-5 (pbk. ed.)
"Greenwillow Books."

18 19 20 21 CG/LSCH 10 9 8 7 6 5 4 3 2 1 First Edition

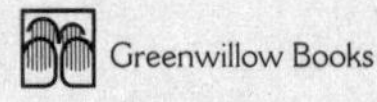

For my treasures—Rosemary, Stan,
Philip, & Margaret—H. P.

For my buddies,
Peyton and Zane—L. A.

Contents

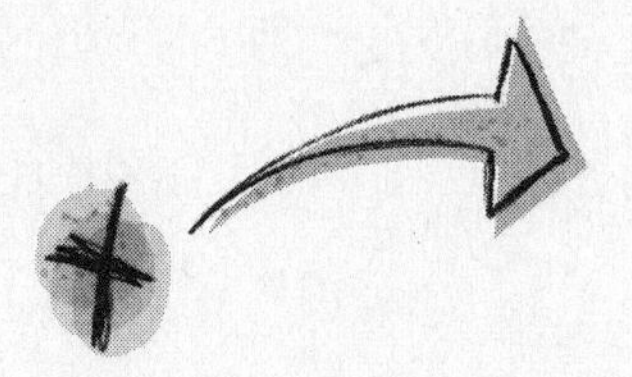

Chapter 1

From Here to There

"Welcome to the Longest Bridge in the World," said Amelia Bedelia's father, glancing in the rearview mirror at Amelia Bedelia and her friend Alice. Their car had been stuck in traffic for a very, very long time.

Alice leaned over to Amelia Bedelia and whispered, "The longest bridge in the world? Says who?"

"Says my dad," said Amelia Bedelia.

"Traffic to the beach is usually backed up," said Amelia Bedelia's mother. "It always takes a long time. Today isn't too bad."

Amelia Bedelia's father lowered his window and breathed in the sea breeze. He shut his eyes, savoring the serenity.

BAAAAAAAAHHNNNN!

The blaring horn of a boat passing under the bridge startled Amelia Bedelia's father.

Amelia Bedelia recognized the boat. "That's the *Reel Busy*," she said. "Captain Will is welcoming us back to the shore."

"Good thing I had my seat belt on," her father said. "I would have gone right through the sunroof."

"We don't have a sunroof," said Amelia Bedelia.

"I would have made one," said her father.

Alice giggled. Amelia Bedelia started to giggle too. Then they couldn't stop. Soon they were laughing so hard, tears were pouring down their

cheeks. Of all the good things that had happened at Camp Echo Woods, becoming friends with Alice was the

best. The only thing that had ever come between them was Amelia Bedelia's dog, Finally, who was snoozing in the middle of the seat.

Amelia Bedelia wiped her eyes and looked out the window. She spotted Blackberry Island in the middle of the bay. Something was different. It looked as though a giant sailboat had run aground. "Hey, Mom," she said. "Look at Blackberry—"

HONK-HONK-HOONNK!!!

Amelia Bedelia's father jumped. He hadn't noticed that the traffic had started moving.

"Keep your shirt on, pal!" he yelled, glancing back at the honker.

"There are two guys in that jeep, Dad," said Amelia Bedelia.

Amelia Bedelia's father shook

his head and began inching forward.

"Neither one has a shirt on," said Amelia Bedelia. "Which one is your pal?

Are you friends with both of them?" She completely forgot to look at Blackberry Island again until the island was out of sight and it was too late. She shrugged, knowing that she'd visit soon enough and figure out the mystery.

"At last!" said Amelia Bedelia's mother

as they drove off the bridge. "Oh! Would you look at this! Isn't that new?"

What had been a square park at the end of the bridge was now a roundabout with cars circling around.

"What a big improvement," said Amelia Bedelia's father. "A traffic circle keeps cars moving."

"If our time on the bridge is shorter, does that make the bridge shorter, too?" said Amelia Bedelia.

"Wait a second," said Alice. "This isn't

the world's longest bridge anymore? No fair!"

One thing that was the same was the *Whereami*. The pint-sized pirate ship was still on display, now in the center of the new circle. Amelia Bedelia pointed out the scorch marks on the wood from the accidental fire that had almost caused the *Whereami* to go up in flames. Amelia

Bedelia told Alice how her cousin, Jason, and his crew of "pirates" had put out the fire by hurling beach balls filled with water at it.

"Jason is older than we are," added Amelia Bedelia.

"I was just about to ask," said Alice.

"I know," said Amelia Bedelia.

Amelia Bedelia and Alice were on the same wavelength. Sometimes talking was unnecessary. It was like they were plugged into each other's brains.

"Does Jason still think he's a pirate?" asked Alice.

"Oh no. His mother says he's moved on," said Amelia Bedelia's mother.

"Now what does Jason want to be? A Viking?" said Alice.

Amelia Bedelia's father snorted and then started to laugh. "Bravo,

Alice!" he said. "Thanks. I needed a good laugh after all that traffic."

Amelia Bedelia's mother's eyebrows were arching so high, they would have gone through the sunroof, if they had had one. Amelia Bedelia could tell she was laughing to herself too.

A block away from Aunt Mary's beach house, Amelia Bedelia's father stopped for some kids who were crossing the road to get to the ocean.

"From pirate to Viking . . . that's quite a career path," said Amelia Bedelia's father.

"Don't be ridiculous, honey," said Amelia Bedelia's mother.

"It makes total sense," said Amelia Bedelia's father. "Pirates and Vikings both cruise around causing havoc and mayhem. That's the job description of every teenage boy."

"Jason isn't like that," said Amelia Bedelia's mother.

"Why don't you just ask him?" said Amelia Bedelia, pointing at the kids in the crosswalk. "Jason's right there, in front of us."

Before Amelia Bedelia's mother could roll down her window, Amelia Bedelia's father leaned on the horn.

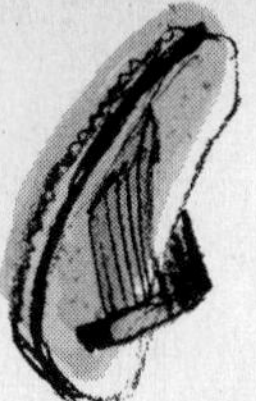

Jason jumped into the air, dropping his towel and surfboard. His flip-flops flew off his feet.

"What? Are you kidding?" said Amelia Bedelia's mother. "Talk about causing mayhem and havoc!" She hopped out of the car, hugged Jason hello, and apologized for honking at him.

Amelia Bedelia, Alice, and Finally got out of the car too. Amelia Bedelia's father drove across the intersection, parked, and hurried back to join them.

"You should have seen your face, Jason," said Amelia Bedelia after she'd introduced her cousin to Alice.

"I jumped right out of my flip-flops," said Jason, laughing.

"Sorry, Jason," said Amelia Bedelia's father. "I wanted to get your attention."

"It worked," said Jason. "I just put some stuff in the beach house, where you're staying—food like milk, eggs, fresh fruit. You know, things that grown-ups worry about. Amelia Bedelia, drop off your bags, then meet me on the beach and we'll go grazing in town."

Chapter 2

A Short Leash

At long last they had arrived at Aunt Mary's beach house. Amelia Bedelia flung open her car door, jumped out, and started stretching.

"Come on, girl, you've been cooped up too long," she said.

"Are you talking to me?" asked Alice.

"I was talking to Finally," said Amelia

Bedelia. "But you can come too. Come on, girl. Come on, Alice!"

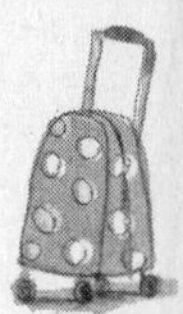

Alice started chasing Amelia Bedelia around the car. Then Finally started chasing Alice and Amelia Bedelia around the yard.

"Don't ask me to scratch behind your ears, Alice!" yelled Amelia Bedelia. The friends (and Finally) kept dodging Amelia

Bedelia's father as he unpacked the car and carried things into the house.

BONK!

"Yeow!" yelled Amelia Bedelia's father. "Ow! Owie!"

Amelia Bedelia and Alice found him bending over, cradling the back of his head with both hands and rubbing it as hard as he could.

"What are you doing, Dad?" asked Amelia Bedelia.

Finally licked his face and whined.

"I'm seeing stars," he said.

"Where?" asked Amelia Bedelia, looking around for famous faces.

"Stars like in cartoons, when someone gets whacked

on the head," he said.

"So right this minute, little planets and chirping birds are circling your head?" asked Amelia Bedelia.

"Ouch!" said Alice. "That must hurt."

"Tell me about it," said her father.

"She just did," said Amelia Bedelia.

"Honey, are you okay?" said Amelia Bedelia's mother, running to his side. "I heard you holler. The whole town heard. Where does it hurt?"

Amelia Bedelia's father pointed at the trunk lid with one hand and to the back of his head with the other.

"Oww-wow-wow! What a nasty lump," Amelia Bedelia's mother said, giving that spot a kiss.

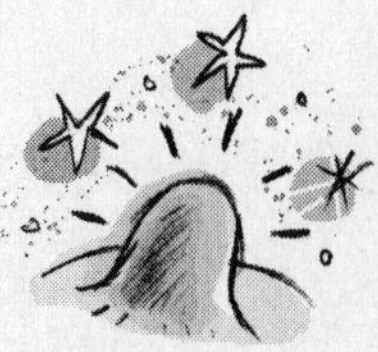

"You're never too old to get a boo-boo kissed," whispered Alice to Amelia Bedelia.

Amelia Bedelia nodded. "My mom always makes me feel better. Her kiss cures cuts and scrapes, bumps and bruises, nosebleeds and burns, splinters, blisters, insect bites. . . ."

"So far, this vacation has been a headache," said Amelia Bedelia's father.

"Well, we're here for two weeks," said Amelia Bedelia's mother. "We can like it or lump it. . . . I think we—"

"Dad, you already lumped it," said Amelia Bedelia, pointing at his head.

"Now let's like it," said Alice.

Amelia Bedelia's father looked from one girl to the other. "No wonder you two get along," he said.

"Let's get you some ice," said Amelia Bedelia's mother, leading him inside.

Amelia Bedelia and Alice finished unpacking the car. They hauled their bags to their room.

"My cousin Jason and I shared this room last summer," said Amelia Bedelia.

"Reminds me of camp," said Alice, flipping a coin in the air. "Call it."

"Heads," said Amelia Bedelia.

"You win," said Alice. "I'll take the bottom bunk."

"Just like camp," said Amelia Bedelia.

The girls investigated the room. Jason had taken everything to the cottage on Blackberry Island. Everything except a map from *Treasure Island* that was still taped to the wall. Amelia Bedelia stared at the letter X on the map, showing where the treasure was buried on that island.

"Is that the island Jason moved to?" asked Alice.

"No, this map is from his favorite book, *Treasure Island*," said Amelia Bedelia. "Jason lives on Blackberry Island now."

"Did it come with buried treasure?" said Alice.

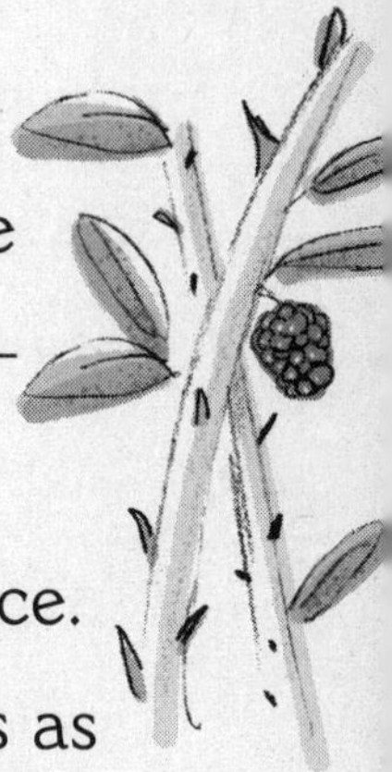

"Blackberry Island?" said Amelia Bedelia. "No, the only treasure there is growing right behind his house—billions of ripe blackberries."

"Yum, I can't wait," said Alice.

"They're guarded by thorns as big as shark fins and as sharp as shark teeth," said Amelia Bedelia.

"Never mind," said Alice.

POP-pop-poppity-POP! came the sound of popcorn in the making. The girls

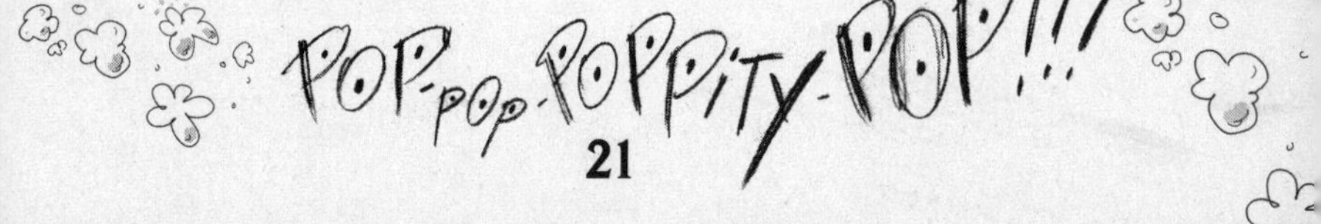

POP-pop-POPPITY-POP!!!

changed quickly into their suits and ran through the kitchen, grabbing handfuls of warm popcorn on their way out the back door.

"How about lunch, ladies?" asked Amelia Bedelia's mother.

"We're eating with Jason," said Amelia Bedelia. "We're meeting him at the beach, then going downtown."

"Come home soon," said her mother. "Aunt Mary left us this popcorn with a note saying she'd pop over later."

"Glad we didn't have to wait for her to start popping," said Amelia Bedelia, grabbing another handful. "It's delicious!"

Amelia Bedelia and Alice headed to the beach, with Finally racing ahead and tugging on her leash. As soon as they crossed over the dune, Amelia Bedelia

unclipped Finally. The three girls were so happy to be running free and feeling the soft sand between their toes.

Amelia Bedelia saw a group of surfers offshore. She spotted Jason sitting on his board, bobbing up and down on the ocean swells. She and Alice waved to him. He waved back, then started paddling like mad toward the beach. He stood up on his board, caught the crest of a big wave, and rode it all the way to shore.

Amelia Bedelia and Alice applauded. "That was amazing!" said Amelia Bedelia. "Last summer you watched the surfers. Now you are one."

"You can learn too," said Jason. "I'll set you up with the works."

"Works? No thanks! We're on vacation," said Amelia Bedelia. "Our only work is to relax."

"Spoken like a true surfer," said Jason. "You've already got the right attitude. I'll get boards for both of you and leashes and—"

"Leashes? We're not wearing leashes!" said Amelia Bedelia.

"Second time today I've been called a dog," said Alice.

"Trust me," said Jason. "The leash

is for your surfboard, not you. It attaches around your ankle and it's pretty short, so you don't have to swim after your board if you fall off."

Amelia Bedelia snapped the dog leash back on Finally.

"I know," said Jason, "let's go get lunch and then we'll get your gear."

Chapter 3

Really Jolly Roger

Amelia Bedelia, Alice, Jason, and Finally walked down Main Street.

"It seems like a lot has changed," said Amelia Bedelia.

"That's new," said Jason, pointing at a sign. "This miniature golf course used to be called Sea Breeze Fairways. The holes and obstacles were about the beach.

Now it's all about pirates. The windmill with moving blades is now a ship's wheel. Get a hole in one, you get a free eye patch."

"Look," said Alice. "It's the home of the Yo-Ho-Hole in One!"

"After we put out the fire on the *Whereami*, buccaneers were big," said Jason. "Pirates were popping up everywhere."

"Even mini golf?" said Amelia Bedelia.

"I can't blame them," said Jason. "Beach businesses have only a couple of months to make most of their money for the whole year."

"They've got to eat," said Alice.

"So do we. I'm starving," said Jason.

The sidewalk was getting more crowded the closer they got to town. They saw lots of Jason's friends from last summer, kids who worked downtown during the day but were in Jason's pirate crew at night. Some kids still called Jason by his pirate name, "Captain J."

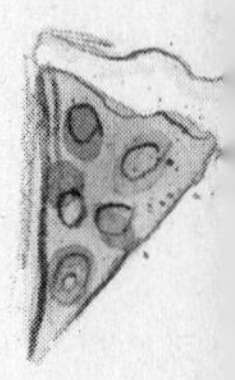

Jason's friends mostly worked at snack shops and food carts, and they treated Amelia Bedelia, Alice, and Jason to goodies, from pizza to ice cream. Alice

loved the ramen from a new place called Oodles of Noodles. Amelia Bedelia even ate the second corn dog of her life, sharing it with Alice.

Some shops put out bowls of doggie treats and cool water. Finally was in heaven, hanging out with other dogs, barking and sniffing and yipping and yapping. The dogs were friendly, the tourists were friendly, and everyone was friendly to Jason.

"Jason, you should run for mayor," said Alice.

"I told him that last summer," said Amelia Bedelia.

"You know everybody. Everyone likes

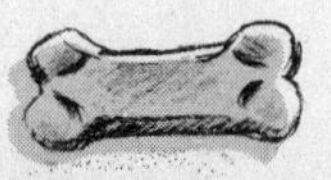

you," said Alice. "Even the dogs would vote for you."

"Thanks," said Jason, scratching Finally behind her ears. "I'll think about it. But right now let's go meet my friend Roger for your first surfing lesson."

"Is your Roger a Jolly Roger?" asked Amelia Bedelia.

"Really jolly. Happiest guy I know," said Jason. "Before he discovered surfing, he used to be miserable. We nicknamed him Notso, because he was Not So Jolly Roger."

Amelia Bedelia shook her head, just

thinking about meeting this used-to-be-crabby surfer named Jolly Roger.

"That must be the place," said Alice, laughing.

Jason stopped in front of a shop just off the main drag.

"Curl City," said Amelia Bedelia, reading the sign. "Is this a hairdresser?"

"Surf Shoppee?" said Alice, rolling her

P-p-e-e

eyes. "P-p-e-e?"

"I hope Roger surfs better than he spells," said Amelia Bedelia.

"He's the best," said Jason.

Just then, the door swung open so fast, it slammed back against the wall of the shop.

BANG!

Amelia Bedelia and Alice jumped. Finally barked. A guy bounded out with open arms.

"Captain J! Long time no see!" he shouted.

"Roger, my man," said Jason. "Jollier than ever."

They kept hugging, slapping backs, until Roger noticed Amelia Bedelia, Alice, and Finally.

"Who are these groms?" he asked.

Jason introduced Roger to the girls and Finally.

"Do you like my sign?" asked Roger. "It's old-timey, right?"

"We like it," said Alice. "It sure got our attention."

"That's its job," said Amelia Bedelia.

"Honestly, it's so bad it's cool," said Jason.

"Okay, let's get you boards and leashes," said Roger. "Then we'll head to the beach for a dry run."

"Why dry?" asked Amelia Bedelia. "Don't we need water?"

"It's easier to learn the basics on land first," said Roger. "Then we'll do a wet run, groms."

"What did you call us?" asked Alice.

"Grommet. Grom for short," said Roger. "It's not an insult. It's slang for a young surfer, like you two. Let's go, groms!"

Chapter 4

Surf's Up!

Amelia Bedelia and Alice carried their boards out to the beach and put them down on the sand. Roger set his board in front of theirs, so they could see what he was doing. Jason headed off into the waves with his surfboard while Finally dug a hole in the sand.

stringer

“That skinny line running down the center of every surfboard is called the stringer,” Roger said. “Stand in the middle of your board, your left foot forward, right foot back. The stringer should run right under the arches of your feet.”

Amelia Bedelia did just what he said. When she looked over at Alice, it was like seeing a mirror image of herself. Alice was standing with her right foot forward and her left foot back.

“Alice, the way you’re standing is called goofy foot,” said Roger. “Switch your feet.”

“Can I stay like this?” asked Alice. “I learned how to snowboard this way. I’m used to it.”

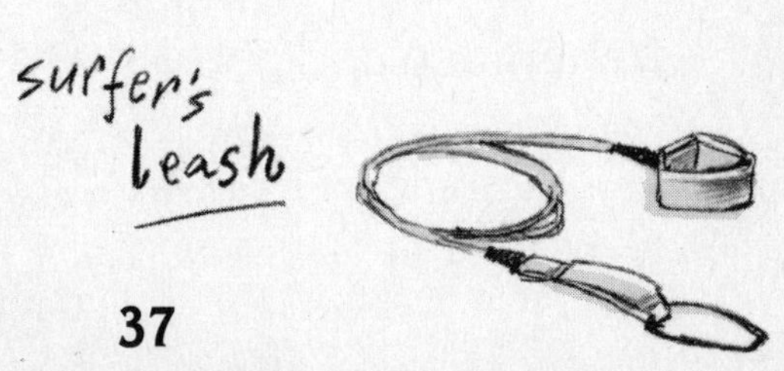

"Roger!" said Roger.

Alice laughed and kept her right foot forward, her left foot back.

Amelia Bedelia laughed and kept her left foot forward, her right foot back.

"Okay. Here's my secret to being a good surfer," said Roger. "Gather around."

Amelia Bedelia and Alice hopped off their boards and started walking toward Roger. Amelia Bedelia tripped, landing flat on her face and getting a mouthful of sand.

"Amelia Bedelia, you don't have to attach the leash to your ankle yet," said Roger. "We're on land. Your board won't float away."

"Yeah, I'm the goofy foot, not you," said Alice.

Roger stretched out on his board, on his stomach.

"The key to surfing is being able to pop up on your board," said Roger. He placed his hands on the board, on either side of his chest.

"First, push up," he said, doing a push-up and holding it for a second.

"Then pop up," he said, scooting both feet forward and tucking them under his body.

"Then look up," he said, looking straight ahead.

"Now stand up, but stay low."

Roger repeated the whole thing in one swift motion.

"It's almost like dancing," said Amelia Bedelia.

"Very smooth," said Alice.

"Your turn," said Roger.

Amelia Bedelia and Alice lay facedown on their boards.

"Push up. Pop up. Look up. Stand up," said Roger. "Think *up*! Like surf's up!"

The girls were a little ragged, but they did it.

"Excellent! Again!" said Roger. "Push up. Pop up. Look up. Stand up. Once

Roger's Pop-Up Torture Test

1. Push Up!
2. Pop Up!
3. Look Up!
4. Stand Up!

*REPEAT until your legs are SCREAMING for MERCY!

again. Push up. Pop up. Look up. Stand up. Again! Looking good, groms!"

Amelia Bedelia wished she'd counted how many times they did Roger's Pop-Up Torture Test. Her leg muscles were screaming for mercy.

"Now you're getting the idea," said Roger. "But this time, pop up as fast as you can."

"If I pop up one more time, I'm going to throw up," said Alice.

"We just came from lunch," said Amelia Bedelia. "Corn dogs."

"Got it," said Roger. "I don't want you getting sick or getting sick of surfing before you catch your first wave. Let's head into the water."

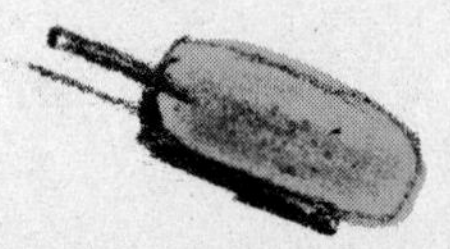

With tiny waves lapping against their ankles, Amelia Bedelia and Alice followed Roger into the ocean. Finally raced back and forth along the frothy edge of the surf.

"Which ankle does the leash go on?" asked Amelia Bedelia.

"The right one," said Roger.

"Which ankle is the right one?" said Amelia Bedelia.

"Your right ankle is right, because your right foot is back," said Roger. "Otherwise you'll get tangled in your leash."

Alice attached her leash to her left ankle.

"Good thinking, Goofy," said Roger. "These waves are ankle busters. But you can practice popping up."

"Do surfers exaggerate everything?" asked Alice.

"If possible," said Roger.

Amelia Bedelia giggled. Then Alice giggled. Then they both started to laugh.

"When a wave comes that you want to ride," said Roger. "Paddle as fast as you can until it's right behind you. Then pop up, pushing your board down into the water and scooting your feet under you."

They practiced popping up five more times.

"You got it," he said. "Here's a tip that took me forever to learn: do not look down at your board. It's there. Otherwise you wouldn't be floating. Look straight ahead. Look at where you want to go."

Jason jogged down the beach carrying his board. He grabbed Finally's leash and

scratched her ear. "Sorry about these puny waves," he called. "Tomorrow morning we'll head to Point Pointless."

"Pointless?" said Alice. "That doesn't sound promising."

"It was called the Point," said Roger. "But during the winter, the point of land fell into the ocean during a big storm. It may be pointless, but now it has the best surf."

"I just hope it isn't the Point of No Return," said Amelia Bedelia.

Chapter 5

Wiped Out

Tap-tap-tap. There it was again, a glasspecker tapping at her window. Amelia Bedelia knew she was dreaming, but that glasspecker kept tapping, as annoying and persistent as its cousin, the woodpecker.

Amelia Bedelia sat straight up in bed.

"That's Jason," she said. She jumped out of bed, ran to the window, and opened it before Jason could tap again.

"Surf's up," said Jason.

"I'm not," said Amelia Bedelia.

"Jason, do you ever sleep?" asked Alice from the bottom bunk. "Go away or we won't vote for you for mayor."

There was a knock at their door.

"You guys awake?" said Amelia Bedelia's father. "Jason is outside."

"We know, we know," said Amelia Bedelia.

"Time and tide wait for no man," said her father.

"Dad, we're girls," said Amelia Bedelia.

Alice got out of bed like a stiff-legged zombie.

"Oh! Owww! OHHH! Ouch! Owwie!" she cried.

Oh! Owww! OHHH!

Ouch! Owwie!

"What's wrong?" asked Amelia Bedelia as she climbed down from the top bunk. "OH! OWWIE!"

Every muscle was sore from all that popping up!

Jason and Roger were waiting in the kitchen.

"What's up?" said Roger.

"You're up. We're up," said Amelia Bedelia.

"I'm barely up," said Alice.

"Surf's up," said Jason. "I brought you wetsuits."

"Are you serious?" said Amelia Bedelia. "We're freezing and you want us to put on wet suits?"

"They're made out of rubber," said Jason. "You'll be way warmer."

As they walked to Point Pointless in their wetsuits, Amelia Bedelia kept glancing at the ocean. The waves were huge, crashing so loudly that it was impossible to hear anything else. It was pretty,

though. And the sky was pink.

"We're in luck!" yelled Roger. "There's a storm way out at sea, making the waves bigger than usual. Plus the tide's coming in. Later today these might be the biggest waves of the summer!"

Amelia Bedelia was not ready for this. It reminded her of the one time she had tried skateboarding, and ended up crashing into a fountain at the park.

"Just do what I do," said Jason, waxing her board after she'd attached her leash. "Follow me."

Amelia Bedelia copied him. She did a perfect duck dive, getting past the

incoming waves. The four of them gathered offshore, bobbing in a lineup. It was quieter now, and almost peaceful.

Amelia Bedelia looked at the beach. The seagulls were swooping, other surfers were arriving, and the lifeguards manned their big chairs. Roger took off first, then Alice.

"You're up," said Jason. "I'll follow you."

Amelia Bedelia started

paddling like mad. She felt a wave lifting the back of her board, pushing her in the direction of the beach. Putting everything into her pop-up, she found herself in a crouch, staring at the shore. Surfing! Was she really surfing? She looked down at her feet on the board. . . .

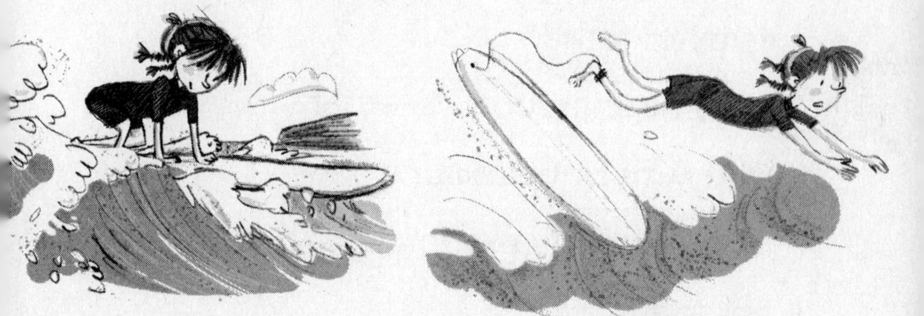

Amelia Bedelia dragged herself through the front door just as her parents were making breakfast. Even though she never drank coffee, Amelia Bedelia liked the way it smelled when it was

brewing. It smelled like home.

"Are you okay, sweetie? Where's Alice?" asked Amelia Bedelia's mother.

"Still surfing," said Amelia Bedelia. "She's with Roger and Jason."

"I didn't know she knew how to surf," said her father.

"She snowboards—that's like surfing," said Amelia Bedelia.

"Just add a mountain with snow," said her father.

"Alice doesn't strike me as the surfing type," said her mother. "But still waters run deep."

"Mom, we were in the ocean," said Amelia Bedelia.

"There was nothing still about that water."

"Isn't it fun to hit the beach at dawn?" asked her father.

"It was until the beach hit back," said Amelia Bedelia. "I was doing great, and then I looked down. *Splat.* I went face-first into the sand, skinned my knees, my elbow, my—"

"Oh, sweetie," said Amelia Bedelia's mother. "Let me see."

"Sounds like you already had surf and turf for breakfast," said her father. "How about eggs and bacon?"

"Thanks, Daddy," said Amelia Bedelia.

"What kind of eggs do you feel like?" asked her father.

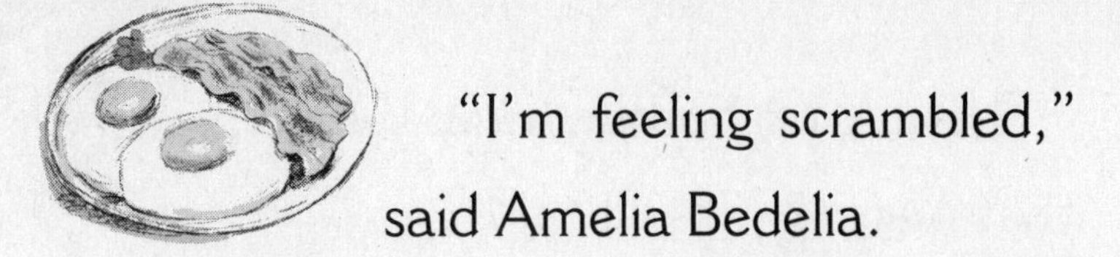

"I'm feeling scrambled," said Amelia Bedelia.

"You look it," said her father. "Keep your sunny side up while I get cracking."

Amelia Bedelia's father went to work, pulling breakfast together while Amelia Bedelia took a quick turn in the outdoor shower to rinse the sand off. Then her mother put on a few Band-Aids. At last Amelia Bedelia snuggled with Finally and drank hot chocolate. She was just tucking into her eggs when Alice staggered in. Amelia Bedelia's father cracked a couple more eggs.

"Pearl called while you were out," said Amelia Bedelia's mother. "She's taking a quick sail around the bay this afternoon.

She was wondering if you two would like to come along."

Even though she was totally exhausted and sore, Amelia Bedelia perked up. She'd been looking forward to this moment and dreading it at the same time. She liked both Alice and Pearl so much. But what if they didn't like each other? What if they didn't get along? Amelia Bedelia had heard the saying "Two's company and three's a crowd."

That afternoon, after a long nap and a little lunch, Amelia Bedelia and Alice headed down to the marina where Pearl kept her boat.

"There she is!" Amelia Bedelia said to Alice, pointing out the tall girl with the curly blond ponytail standing on the pier.

"Pearl!" yelled Amelia Bedelia. "Hi! It's great to see you! This is my friend Alice."

"Hi, Alice," said Pearl. "Welcome to the shore."

"Weird. I just noticed you guys are the same height," said Amelia Bedelia. "So you can see eye to eye."

"I sure hope so," said Pearl.

"That would be great," said Alice.

Having two best friends sure takes work, thought Amelia Bedelia as the three girls climbed aboard Pearl's sailboat. But with Pearl and Alice, it was worth it. So far, so good!

"Alice and I went sailing every day for eight weeks at camp," said Amelia Bedelia.

"Lucky! Well, in that case, you two can take over while I relax," said Pearl. She leaned back, looked up at the sky, and said, "Red sky in morning, sailors take warning. Red sky at night, sailor's delight."

"What happens if there's a red sky in the morning like today, and there's also a red sky at night?" said Alice.

Good question, thought Amelia Bedelia. She looked at Pearl, wondering what seafaring wisdom she would impart. Pearl knew a lot about sailing and being on the water.

"There's only one thing to do," said Pearl. "Stay home and hide under the covers."

When they finally stopped laughing, Pearl said, "Hand me that line, please."

"This one?" said Amelia Bedelia, handing it to her.

"Why that one?" asked Alice.

"A line is a piece of rope with a job to do, " said Pearl. "The job of this line is to hold us to the pier on Blackberry Island."

Pearl made a loop and then tied a knot to hold the loop and gave it to the girls to examine.

"This is a bowline," she said. "That loop will never slip and never get tighter. That's why it's used to rescue people."

"In case you didn't hide under the covers in time?" said Alice.

"Like us," said Amelia Bedelia.

Chapter 6

"One Man's Trash . . ."

The annual Beach Ball was coming soon. Amelia Bedelia's aunt Mary and her new husband, Bob, decided to have a cookout at their new home on Blackberry Island before the festivities kicked off.

Alice and Amelia Bedelia were sailing

over to the island with Pearl. While Pearl sailed, Amelia Bedelia and Alice practiced tying different knots, including a bowline.

Amelia Bedelia's parents, Jason, and Finally were riding to the island in a speedboat. Amelia Bedelia watched them fly by. Finally's ears looked like furry flags, flapping in the breeze.

Naturally, the speedboat beat the sailboat to the island. After tying up at the pier, the girls walked to the cottage. Aunt Mary was handing out glasses of homemade lemonade.

"I'll give you the fifty-cent tour before dinner," she said.

"Do you have change for a dollar?" asked Amelia Bedelia.

"You can owe me," said Mary with a laugh. She led everyone through the house, pointing out improvements and additions that had made the historic place cozy and livable again.

"These floors are original to the cottage," said Mary. "See how wide the planks are?"

"These pieces of oak could be from an old ship," said Bob.

"That's so cool," said Alice.

Amelia Bedelia was amazed to see

all the changes. "Wow, this place was a wreck the last time I saw it," she said.

"Now it's a jewel," said Amelia Bedelia's mother. "Honey, when can we get a second house?"

"Right after we pay for our first house," said Amelia Bedelia's father.

"Right you are," said Bob. "A second home can be a money pit. This one has cost plenty.

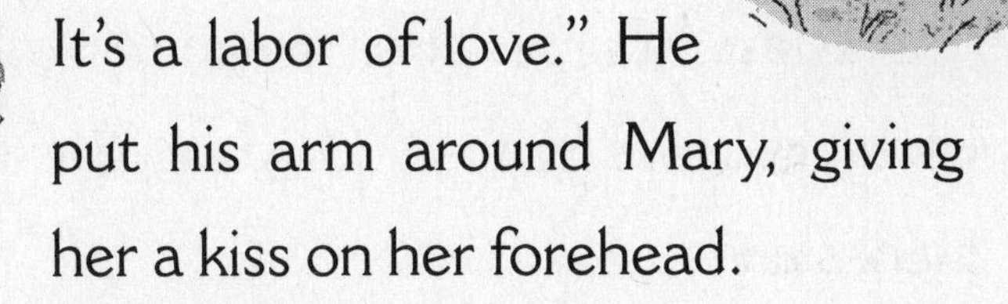

It's a labor of love." He put his arm around Mary, giving her a kiss on her forehead.

Amelia Bedelia's mother pointed at Bob and Mary. "See that?" she said. "They call that being romantic."

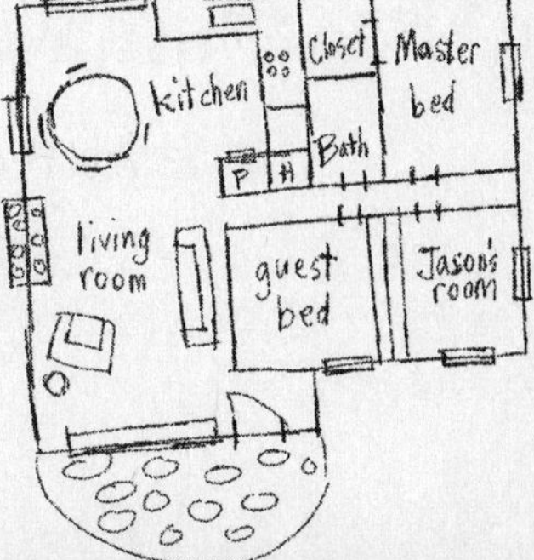

"Who is *they*?" asked Amelia Bedelia. "They who?"

Amelia Bedelia's father put his arm around Amelia Bedelia's mother and planted a kiss on her cheek.

"That's a start," she said.

"Remember Bob's niece, Anita? She was our architect," said Mary. "She designed everything. She did a wonderful job."

"Want to check out my room?" said Jason, opening his door and inviting them in. All three girls shrieked at the huge windows.

"Wow!" said Alice.

"It's like being on a boat in the bay," said Pearl.

"All you need is this," said

Amelia Bedelia, handing Jason the rolled-up piece of paper she was carrying.

"*Treasure Island!*" said Jason, unfurling it. "I was wondering where this map was."

"You left it in your old bedroom," said Amelia Bedelia. "But it belongs here."

"Ladies and gentlemen, we've come to the last stop on our tour, the living room!" Mary was pretending to hold a microphone and making her voice sound louder than usual.

Bob stopped what he was doing in the kitchen and came to join them. "Take a look at our newest work of art," he said, pointing at a huge gold frame above the fireplace.

Amelia Bedelia whispered to Jason, "If it's new, does that make it modern art?"

Jason smiled, shaking his head. "No, it's just new to us. It's actually really old."

They all stared at the frame. Ornate carving surrounded a square space. In the center, mounted on ocean-blue velvet, was a crumpled piece of parchment. Its edges were tattered, one corner was torn, and a brown stain spread across the bottom. Everyone was quiet until Amelia

Bedelia's father spoke up.

"Okay, Bob. I give up. Why did you frame a piece of trash?"

"One man's trash is another man's treasure," said Bob. "Isn't that what they say?"

"They're back again!" said Amelia Bedelia. "But who are *they*?"

"If I saw that on the street, I'd walk by it," said Amelia Bedelia's mother.

"Mom!" said Amelia Bedelia. "That would make you a litterbug."

Her mother blushed. "You're right. I'd pick it up and toss it in the trash," she said.

"Anita did some research before starting our renovation," said Bob. "She was looking through old family papers when she stumbled upon that scrap."

"Ow!" said Amelia Bedelia. "Was she hurt?"

"No, she was happy," said Bob, smiling. "That piece of paper was scrunched up in the bottom of a box. No one thought it was important or paid any attention to it. That's probably why it survived."

"So what is it?" said Amelia Bedelia's father.

"It's a map, maybe the first map made of this area," said Bob.

He took down the frame. Everyone gathered around him to get a closer look.

"Look! No town. No houses," said Bob. "See how much the coastline has changed? This is the bay. The bridge goes from here to here. Only one thing stayed the same. Look familiar?" He was pointing at an irregular speck of land in the center of the bay.

"Blackberry Island!" said Pearl.

"Bingo," said Bob.

"Let's play bingo later," said Amelia Bedelia. "Tell us more about the map."

"I'm just guessing, but this map must have been drawn by one of my ancestors," said Bob. "Perhaps to stake a claim to this island."

"Back then, not many people could read or write or even sign their names," said Mary. "So the X could mean that the island was claimed by Bob's family a very long time ago."

Amelia Bedelia's heart was racing. Her knees got weaker and weaker. She looked around the room, from one person to the other.

Did I hear right? she wondered. *Let's see,* she thought. *In a place swarming with pirates, someone finds an old map of an island with an X on it.* Was she the only one who got what that meant? Her brain screamed, *Wake up, Jason! You're the* Treasure Island *expert!* Hadn't something amazing just happened?

Amelia Bedelia couldn't hold it in any

longer. "Is that where the  pirate buried his treasure?" she blurted out.

There was silence. Then everyone burst out laughing, even Jason.

"What a vivid imagination," said Mary. "You're the treasure, Amelia Bedelia."

"If anyone could find buried treasure, it's Metal Man Bob, right?" said Amelia Bedelia's father.

"Yeah," said Jason. "That X is right in our backyard."

"Wish it were true, Amelia Bedelia," said Bob. "But I've combed every inch of this island with my metal detector. Never heard a peep."

"I'm sorry," said

Amelia Bedelia. "I didn't mean to call your ancestor a pirate."

"That's okay," said Bob. "Makes a nice story around the campfire."

"Speaking of campfires, you should get grilling, Bob," said Mary. "These folks must be starving."

Chapter 7

Kitchen or Cave?

Amelia Bedelia's father, Bob, and Jason went outside to light the fire pit. Amelia Bedelia's mother and her aunt Mary headed into the kitchen.

"Would you like me to make my mother's secret salad-dressing recipe?" asked Pearl.

"You bet," said Amelia Bedelia's mother.

"What can Alice and I do, Aunt Mary?" asked Amelia Bedelia.

"Please take the meat and fish out to Uncle Bob," said Mary. "It's on those platters right over there. And thank you!"

Amelia Bedelia and Alice arrived at the fire pit just as the last match sputtered out.

"Dang it," said Bob. "Hey, Jason, run and get us more matches, please."

"Today you run for matches, tomorrow you run for mayor," said Alice.

Jason smiled as he started jogging back to the house.

"Jason's way too young to run for mayor tomorrow," said Amelia Bedelia.

"Well, someday then," said Alice.

Bob and Amelia Bedelia's father kept fussing around with the fire, arranging driftwood and adding dry seaweed.

"Can we help?" said Amelia Bedelia.

"Can you start a fire?" said Bob.

Amelia Bedelia and Alice looked at each other, then back at Bob.

"We're experts," said Alice.

"Over to you, then," said Bob. "Show us your stuff."

Alice arranged a small cone of sticks around a ball of dried grass that Amelia Bedelia had gathered. Then she stacked bigger sticks, log-cabin style, around that upside-down cone shape. Spying a piece of flint on the ground, Amelia Bedelia struck it with the handle of a big fork, sending a small shower of sparks into the dried grass. When a wisp of smoke appeared, both girls began blowing on the glowing ember inside. It kept smoking, smoking, smoking, until, at last, it burst into flames.

"You did it!" hollered Amelia Bedelia's father, bursting into applause.

Bob stuck his fingers in his mouth and let out a whistle

almost louder than the horn on the *Reel Busy*.

"Thank you, thank you," said Jason, who was just arriving with the matches. He put his hands in the air in triumph, basking in their praise. "This meeting of the Jason Fan Club will now come to order," he said. Then he saw the fire that Alice and Amelia Bedelia had started. "Well, it looks like you don't need my matches," said Jason. "Or me! Boo-hoo-hoo!"

His fake crying made the girls laugh.

"Don't put out our fire with your tears," said Amelia Bedelia.

As Bob and Amelia Bedelia's father tended to the fire and

began grilling, Amelia Bedelia recalled a conversation she had overheard last summer. Her mother and Aunt Mary had been talking about cookouts.

"Having a backyard barbecue is like going back twenty thousand years," Aunt Mary had said. "We might as well be eating mastodon burgers and saber-toothed tiger steaks."

"Who wants to cook over a fire, like cavemen?" Amelia Bedelia's mother had replied.

"The gatherers get stuck in the kitchen, struggling to make salads and vegetables exciting," said Aunt Mary. "Meanwhile, the hunters are standing around a fire, grilling and laughing and swapping stories."

"Oh, don't I know," Amelia Bedelia's mother had said. "The only hunting my husband does is rummaging through our freezer for a pint of rocky road ice cream."

Amelia Bedelia looked around at this barbecue. The steaks and fish sizzled, the aromas of food and smoke mingled with the talking and laughter. The breeze was soft, and she could see the bay sparkling through the trees. For Amelia Bedelia, the lesson was crystal clear. Hanging out and grilling around a fire pit was way more fun than being stuck inside a kitchen. At least at the shore!

Chapter 8

$1 + an + Ear = Buccaneer

"Let's shift most of the fire to one side," said Amelia Bedelia's father. "That way we can cook over the hot coals here and use that spot over there to keep things warm until everything is ready."

"Great idea," said Bob. "You're a beach barbecue expert."

"Not really," said Amelia Bedelia's father. "But I once worked with a guy who created a barbecue sauce. I read lots of books and articles about barbecuing while I was figuring out how to sell that sauce."

"In *Treasure Island*, Long John Silver's nickname was Barbecue," said Jason. "He became the ship's cook after his leg was shot off by a cannonball."

"Ouch!" said Alice. "That must have hurt."

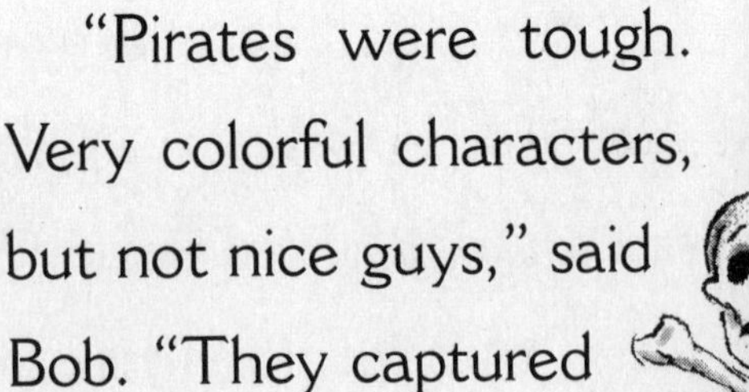

"Pirates were tough. Very colorful characters, but not nice guys," said Bob. "They captured

ships, stole cargo. . . ."

"Took the crew and passengers prisoner," said Jason. "People who didn't have money or jewelry were held for ransom until their family paid up."

"How much?" asked Amelia Bedelia.

"The going rate then was two dollars per person, or a dollar an ear," said Amelia Bedelia's father. "That's why pirates were called buccaneers."

"No kidding," said Alice. Then she noticed the others smiling.

"Yes. Kidding," said Amelia Bedelia.

They all started laughing, even Amelia Bedelia. "Sorry, Alice," she said. "I'm used to my dad joking around and making up stuff that sounds sort of true."

"Buccaneers? Truly the worst joke I've ever heard," said Bob, shaking his head and chuckling.

They were still laughing when Amelia Bedelia's mother arrived carrying a big paper bag. Amelia Bedelia could tell that her mother was thinking about cavemen clowning around while they cooked.

"I hate to interrupt with some actual work, but can you guys grill some ears?" she said.

"Mom! Gross!" said Amelia Bedelia.

"Of corn. Ears of corn," said her mother. "Can you roast them?"

"Sure, honey. But it'll cost you," said Amelia Bedelia's father.

"Cost me?" she asked. "How much?"

"A buck an ear," he said.

They all started laughing again—even Alice. Amelia Bedelia's mother was busy heaping up the platters with their barbecued meats and fish and making room on the fire pit's grill for the corn. She handed one platter to Amelia Bedelia, another to Alice, and grabbed one herself.

"Let's carry these back to the kitchen," she said.

Turning to go, Amelia Bedelia was

sorry to miss more stories around the fire pit. The last thing she heard was Bob saying, "This place is so peaceful now. Hard to believe it was once a pirate stomping ground."

On their way back to the house, Amelia Bedelia began imagining pirates and buccaneers everywhere. They could be lurking behind every clump of grass or tree. What if one jumped out and grabbed her to be ransomed? Would her parents pay up?

She was giving herself the willies just thinking about pirates stomping on this same ground. She started to stomp her feet. That made her feel even more creeped out. A spine-tingling shudder ran through her, so strong that she almost dropped the platter.

"What are you doing?" said Alice.

"Nothing. Just scaring myself out of my wits," said Amelia Bedelia.

The First Grill Masters

Early barbecues were held in the islands of the West Indies, later a haven for pirates. Spanish explorers referred to a *barbacoa*, a framework that the native islanders had taught them to build and use for grilling and smoking meats. Years later, French pirates adapted the same structure, calling it a *boucan*. When a ship sailed near their island, these "boucaners" would row out and attack, armed with the knives they used to butcher meat for grilling. These short, sturdy weapons evolved into the cutlass, a sword favored by pirates for close combat.

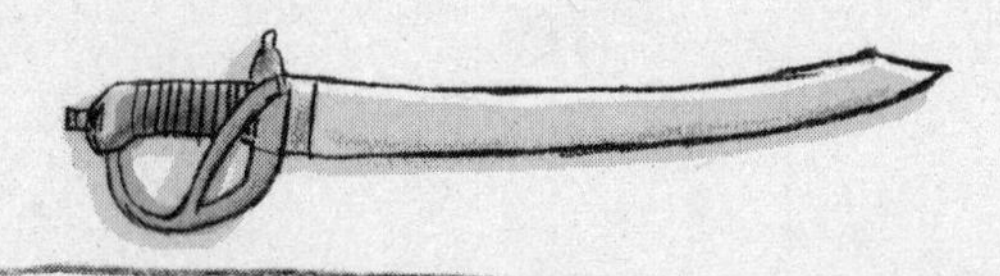

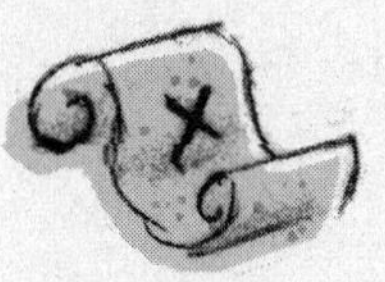

Chapter 9

The Hole Truth

The dining room table was set with eight places, and Aunt Mary was lighting the candles when Amelia Bedelia and Alice walked in with their yummy-smelling platters.

"Oh, I don't know, girls," said Aunt Mary. "Should we eat in or out?"

"Eat out?" said Amelia Bedelia. "We

have all this food and you want to go to a restaurant?"

"I mean inside or outside our house," said Mary.

"I vote for out," said Amelia Bedelia's mother. "We can enjoy the sunset."

"We're eating in, but out," said Mary.

"In. Out. I don't care as long as we eat," said Amelia Bedelia. "I'm hungry!"

Alice and Amelia Bedelia took everything from the dining-room table and reset the picnic table on the patio. Pearl

brought out her salad and dressing, and Aunt Mary and Amelia Bedelia's mother brought out the side dishes and platters just as Amelia Bedelia's father, Bob, and Jason arrived with the roasted corn. There was so much food that Bob set up a smaller table to hold it all, buffet style. Amelia Bedelia's mother closed her eyes, inhaling the delicious aromas.

"Something smells terrific," she said, opening her eyes.

"That would be me," said Amelia Bedelia's father. "Like my new cologne?"

"You smell like a smoky campfire," said Amelia Bedelia.

“That’s the price you pay for hanging around a grill for hours,” said Amelia Bedelia’s mother.

“Amen,” said Amelia Bedelia’s father.

“Yippee!” said Amelia Bedelia. “That’s the shortest grace I’ve ever heard. Let’s eat!”

“That ‘amen’ wasn’t our grace,” said Aunt Mary. “Your dad was just agreeing with your mom.”

“Let’s say the grace we learned at camp,” said Alice.

They all joined hands around the table.

“Now think of something or someone that you are grateful for,” said Alice. “When you are finished, you squeeze the hands of

the people on either side of you."

"That means grace is over," said Amelia Bedelia.

"Then everyone drops their hands," said Alice.

They gave it a try. Everyone loved it.

"I'm thankful you came up with a quick grace," said Jason.

"Let's eat," said Mary. "Dig in!"

Everyone happily did just that.

After a few minutes of serious eating,

Mary added, "And for dessert we're featuring blackberry cobbler."

"Yum!" said Pearl. "Alice, you're going to love Mary's famous blackberry cobbler!"

"Oh, no! Blackberries!" said Mary, shaking her head, her hands on her cheeks. "Why do I always do this?"

"Do what? Bake a fabulous blackberry cobbler?" said Bob.

"You can't help it. You're talented," said Amelia Bedelia's father.

"I forgot my signature final touch," said Mary.

"The whipped cream is right here," said Jason, dipping his finger into the bowl for a taste.

"So what's wrong, Mary?" said Amelia Bedelia's mother.

"I gathered a basket full of fresh blackberries today," said Mary.

"You've got the scratches to prove it," said Bob.

"And I always tell myself, save the biggest and plumpest berries to put on top of each piece, for decoration," said Mary. "But I always wind up using them all in the cobbler."

Everyone was looking at one another and at Mary.

"That's it? That's what's wrong?" said Amelia Bedelia's father. "I was afraid that a crab had crawled into the cobbler and was going to

nibble at our noses."

Even Mary laughed at the thought of that. Standing up, she said, "I'll be back in a sec with more blackberries."

"Hold on, honey," said Bob. "You don't need more scratches. Let one of the kids go."

"I'll get them, Aunt Mary," said Amelia Bedelia.

"You just want to get out of clearing the table," said Jason.

"Shhhh!" said Amelia Bedelia, raising a finger to her lips.

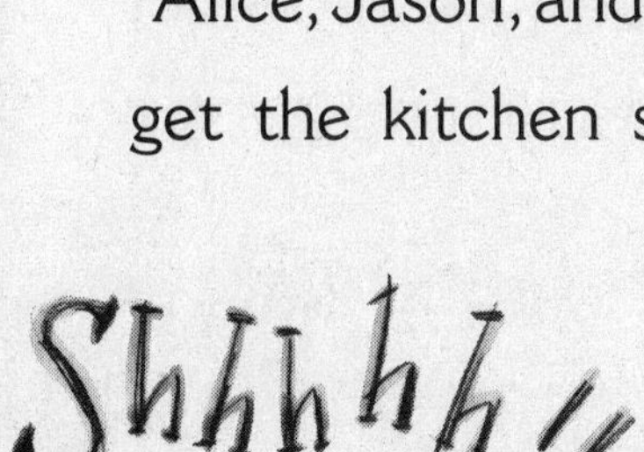

"Thank you, sweetie," said Amelia Bedelia's mother, handing her a basket. "Alice, Jason, and Pearl, you help me. Let's get the kitchen shipshape so we can all enjoy dessert and this beautiful evening."

The sun was just starting to set. Pink, orange, and red rays of light made a glowing path to the berry patch. It was way too pretty for Amelia Bedelia to be scared of pirates.

She ducked down, away from the thorns, and entered the magical circle of berries. Even late in the season, hundreds were still hanging there, plump and ripe.

Amelia Bedelia began picking them as fast as she could. The glossy black berries reflected the sunset, looking like thousands of beady eyes glowing pink and orange and red.

Amelia Bedelia was determined not to let her imagination spook her. *So what if this was a pirate stomping ground?* she told herself. *That was hundreds of years ago.* She could stomp here too. Amelia Bedelia stomped her feet with each berry she picked. One. *Stomp.* Two. *Stomp.* The ground she was stomping on was way too soft and sandy to make a sound. She kept picking and stomping. Seven, *stomp*, eight, *stomp*, nine . . . *CRACK!*

Amelia Bedelia stopped. *What was that?* Turning around, she called out, "Alice, is that you?"

Silence.

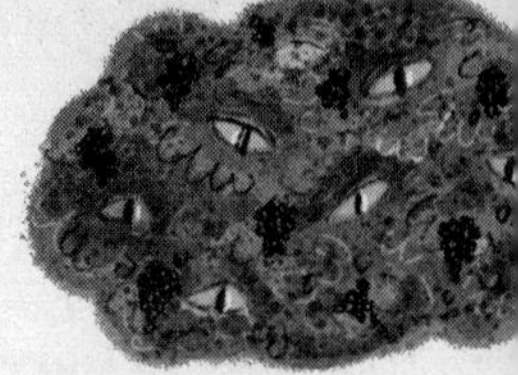

Weird. Amelia Bedelia shivered, then shrugged and kept picking berries. Ten, *stomp*, eleven, *stomp* . . . *CRACK!*

There it was again, this time right under Amelia Bedelia's feet. She looked down. She saw sand disappearing beneath her, swirling. It was like someone had pulled out the stopper of a bathtub full of sand. She was watching it disappearing down the drain. Amelia Bedelia froze. The trickle of sand was

10*, 11*

going faster and faster. Her feet were sinking farther down. The sand was over her ankles, then up her calves, then above her knees. Something was sucking her down a sand drain! She gripped the handle of her basket tighter and hoped that this was not happening to her. Just as she was opening her mouth to holler for help, there came the loudest *CRACK* of all.

Then Amelia Bedelia was plummeting feet-first into Blackberry Island.

Chapter 10

"Where Am I?"

Amelia Bedelia landed on a mound of soft sand. Lying flat on her back and opening her eyes, she found herself looking up at the sky. Actually, it was just a circle of deep blue filling the hole through which she just had fallen.

She saw stars twinkling against the blue. Was she

seeing stars like her father had after hitting his head? No, these stars looked real. And there were no planets circling her head. It must still be early evening.

Amelia Bedelia checked herself out. She wiggled her toes. Check. Wiggled her fingers. Double check. *So far, so good,* she thought. Then she s-l-o-w-l-y sat up and looked around. Luckily, there was still enough light to see. The mound of sand she was sitting on was piled up on a wooden floor. The boards were wide, like in the cottage, but not smooth and shiny like those were.

"Where am I?" she said out loud. Then she laughed. She wasn't afraid or hysterical. She was remembering the legend about the pirate who had stumbled upon this place. He didn't know where he was, so the locals called his ship the *Whereami*.

"I am in the same boat," she said. As her eyes began adjusting to the dim light, she looked around some more. The floor was round, about the same size as her

reading circle at school. The walls had wooden ribs, like the inside of Pearl's sailboat. They curved up, making an arch at a point above her. Or they used to, because that was where she had fallen through. She reached up to try to touch the edge of the hole. It was about three feet higher than her fingers, even on tiptoes. She jumped. No luck. She stumbled over something hard, ending up on her knees in the sand pile. *Great,* she thought. *I look down when I'm surfing, and I fall. I look up when I'm jumping, and I fall.*

"Help!" she yelled. "HELP!" Had she tripped over the berry basket? No, it had rolled against the wall. She picked it up and looked inside.

"A miracle," she said. Five big fat berries were still there. She gobbled them down. "Uh-oh, I should have saved those," she said. "What if they don't find me for days?"

Then a thought crossed her mind. One she was too afraid to say aloud. *What if they don't find me? Ever. Does anybody even miss me?* It suddenly grew darker in the hole. She looked up. Something was blocking the last of the light.

"WOOF!"

"Finally!" Amelia Bedelia yelled. "Good girl!"

Finally was as excited to see her as Amelia Bedelia was to see her dog. Finally whimpered and wiggled, scooting to the edge of the hole. It was clear that she wanted to leap into the hole with Amelia Bedelia.

Holding up one hand, Amelia Bedelia signaled for Finally to stop. "Stay," she said.

Finally stayed.

"Good girl. Now, get Mom!" Amelia Bedelia said. "Go get Dad!"

But Finally didn't leave. She kept scratching at the edge of the hole, making sand rain down. Amelia Bedelia vowed that if she ever got out, she would watch more old movies with Finally. Ones where the dog on the farm leads everyone to the girl who fell off her horse and broke her leg and is stuck fighting off a pack of coyotes until they rescue her. She vowed to take Finally back to puppy school too.

"Amelia Bedelia! Where are you?" a familiar voice called.

"Alice! Be careful!" yelled Amelia Bedelia, looking up at her friend's concerned face. "I fell into a hole. If you hear a cracking sound, run!"

"Stay here, Alice, I'm getting a line from my boat!"

Amelia Bedelia was happy to hear Pearl's voice too. She smiled when Pearl issued another order: "Jason, go back and get the grown-ups."

"Aye-aye, Captain Pearl!" yelled Jason.

Soon Amelia Bedelia's parents were peering down into the hole—and then Bob and Aunt Mary too.

"Sweetie, are you okay?" called her mother.

Aye-Aye!

"Are you hurt?" said her father.

"I'm fine!" called Amelia Bedelia. "This is too weird."

"We should all stand back," said Bob, shining a flashlight around the berry patch. "It appears this isn't solid ground. We might cause a cave-in."

Just then Pearl returned with her rope. She quickly tied a bowline knot at each end and looped one loop over Amelia Bedelia's father.

"You're our anchor man," she said. "Let's lower the other end into the hole to Amelia Bedelia."

"I'm worried about anyone getting near that hole," he said. "We don't want it to collapse."

"Who weighs the least, Jason or Alice?" asked Aunt Mary.

"How about Finally?" asked Pearl.

"That's why you're the captain," said Jason.

Finally took the other end of the line in her mouth, walked over to the hole, and dropped the bowline knot in.

Amelia Bedelia reached up, grabbed

the loop, and put it over her head, then under her arms, so it was snug against her armpits.

"When you're ready, give us a tug!" yelled Pearl. "We'll haul you up!"

Amelia Bedelia took a last look around. She was reaching for the berry basket when she noticed something shiny sticking up out of the sand. "That's what tripped me," she said. It looked like a handle made of metal. She reached for it, tugging the rope by mistake. She'd just gotten hold of the handle when her family and friends began hoisting her up and out of the hole. Her feet were leaving the ground and swinging in the air, but she hung on to it.

As they began pulling harder, Amelia Bedelia tightened her grip. She was almost upside down now, her feet dangling in midair. At last whatever the handle was attached to slid out of the sandpile, slowly at first and then with a *plop*. It was too dark in the hole now to see clearly what it was, but it was heavy. Amelia Bedelia kept hanging on until she cleared the edge of the hole. It was a chest, a little smaller than a mailbox. Grunting, she handed it to Bob.

"Over to you, Metal Man," she said.

Once Amelia Bedelia was sitting safely on the grassy path outside the berry patch, everyone gathered around her to make sure she was all right. Then she got the sloppiest, wettest kiss ever—from Finally, who was nearly as good as her mom at kissing boo-boos.

Chapter 11

". . . Is Another Girl's Treasure."

The evenings on Blackberry Island were chilly. Aunt Mary herded everyone inside and served her cobbler with whipped cream in the living room.

Amelia Bedelia's parents sat on either side of her, hugging their daughter like there was no tomorrow.

"I'm fine, really," said Amelia Bedelia. "I'm as fine as I was when you asked me a minute ago, Mom. I'm okay."

Amelia Bedelia's father didn't say a word. He gave her another hug on top of the twenty or so he'd already given her.

"What did Amelia Bedelia find?" asked Jason. "Who built it?"

"I'm no expert, but it might be a money pit," said Bob.

"Cool!" said Jason.

"That's what you called vacation homes," said Amelia Bedelia.

"Does our money pit have buried treasure in it, honey?" asked Mary.

"It wasn't buried in the ground," said Bob. "This was more like a safe

deposit box, where pirates could store their treasure."

"A buccaneer bank?" asked Jason.

"That's right," said Bob. "Whoever owned the pit probably collected a fee for storing treasure, much like a banker. It was too risky for a pirate to sail around with all his loot. Other pirates would attack to get it. Or your ship could run aground or sink or catch fire."

"This sounds like that pit they found on Oak Island, in Canada," said Alice. "I read about it."

"Pirates in Canada?" said her mother.

"Cool!" said Jason.

Bob took one last bite of his cobbler. Then, grabbing both handles of the chest, he lifted it up and toward him.

"Okay, Amelia Bedelia," he said. "Let's look at what you found."

"I didn't find it," said Amelia Bedelia. "I fell onto it."

"You sure did," said her father.

"Then I stumbled over it," she said.

"Wish I were that lucky," said Bob. "I've been searching all over for something like this my whole life."

"It was right in your own backyard," said Jason. "Marked with an X."

Examining the chest, Bob let out a whistle so low that Finally, curled at Amelia Bedelia's feet, looked up.

"A true craftsman built this," he said. "Using copper sheets so it won't ever rust. Amazing!"

"That's why it lasted," said Mary.

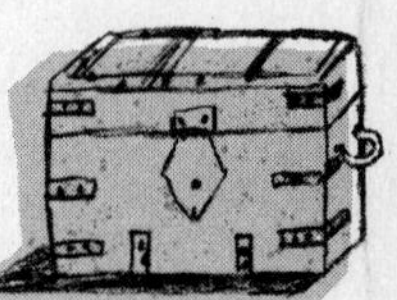

"Looks like the lock rusted away, though," said Pearl. "Salt air gobbles up iron."

"Like it was blackberry cobbler," said Alice, finishing her last forkful.

Bob carefully pried open what was left of the lock and lifted the top. The hinges let out tiny squeals.

Everyone leaned in. What was in this buccaneers' bank?

But instead of immediately rummaging through the chest, Bob took photographs from every angle. "Pictures will help us remember how it was," he said. "It's a record of history."

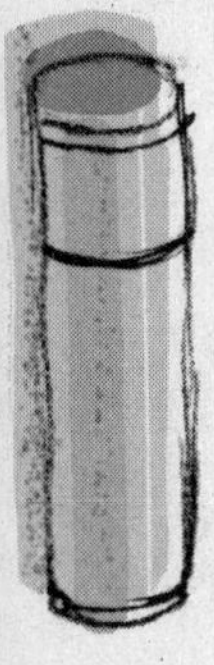

Then he put down his camera and pulled out the biggest thing first, a heavy metal tube. He set it aside, revealing dozens of little rocks, the size and shape of thumbnails. Bob struck one with a camping knife, sending a shower of sparks onto the table.

"Flints were like money then," he said. "Valuable for starting fires and making guns fire. You've heard of flintlock pistols? The sparks from flint ignited the gunpowder in the gun, making it shoot."

gold doubloon

Piece of eight

"Even today, people say fire a gun, even though there's no fire," said Amelia Bedelia's father.

"Look, this one's different," said Amelia Bedelia. Reaching into the box, she pulled out a blackish disk. She dropped it into Bob's hand.

"This is a piece of eight," said Bob.

Amelia looked back in the box. "Where are the other seven pieces?" she asked.

"That's just what this particular coin is called," said Bob. "It's equal to eight reales in the currency of the Spanish Empire. Pirates were always robbing the Spanish Empire."

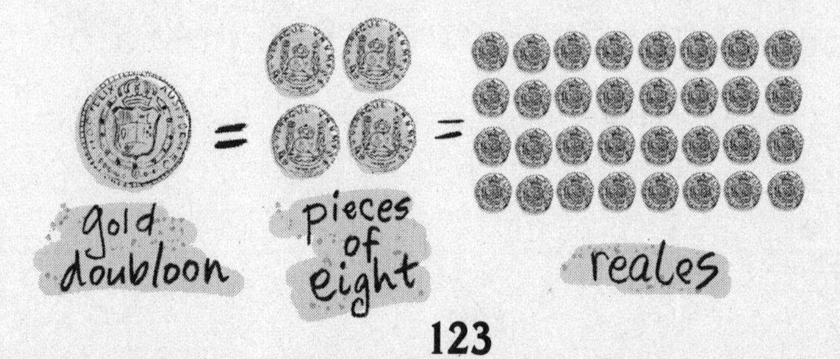

"When they needed change, they would cut that coin into eight pieces," said Amelia Bedelia's father.

"From what I've read, four pieces of eight equal one of those," said Aunt Mary, pointing at the gold doubloon, a gift from Bob, hanging around Jason's neck.

Bob put the piece of eight back in the chest and turned his attention to the brass tube, opening one end.

Out slid another brass tube, with glass at both tips. When Bob pulled on the ends, the tube extended into three

segments, each smaller than the last.

"A spyglass!" shouted Jason.

Looking through the eyepiece at the map above the fireplace, Bob smiled.

"It works too!" he said. "I can see that X from here."

"Me too," said Amelia Bedelia. But she was pointing at the end of the spyglass.

Everyone leaned forward to inspect the spyglass. Sure enough, there was an X scratched on the rim, an X just like the one on the map.

Bob sat back on the sofa and looked at Amelia Bedelia's father. "You work in marketing, right?" he said.

Amelia Bedelia's father nodded.

"If a rumor got out that a pirate treasure

or something old and valuable had been found on this island, what would happen?" asked Bob.

"You'd get lots of company," said Amelia Bedelia's father. "Reporters, photographers, television crews, boats, helicopters, drones with cameras . . ."

"Stop!" said Aunt Mary.

"Can we all join hands again?" asked Bob.

They each took the hands of the person on either side of them, just as they'd done during grace at dinner.

"I'd like us all to promise one thing," said Bob. "Please don't tell anyone about

Amelia Bedelia's discovery—until we're ready to share the news."

Everyone nodded and made a promise to stay silent. The secret of Blackberry Island was safe. Then they all dropped hands.

"Thank you," said Bob.

"Well, this has been another dull cookout," said Aunt Mary.

They all laughed.

"I've had all the excitement I can stand," said Bob. "I'd feel better if you all stayed over and went home in daylight."

"Sleepover!" said Jason. "Excellent!"

"We have plenty of room for everyone," said Aunt Mary.

❒ ❒ ❒

Before the girls headed for the living room to roll out their sleeping bags, Jason put up his map.

"Last summer, I memorized this map," he said. "This summer, I am living it. How amazing is that?"

"It feels weird knowing a real secret," said Amelia Bedelia.

"Not gossip like you hear at school," said Alice.

"This secret could change things forever," said Pearl.

"Were you scared, Amelia Bedelia?" asked Alice.

"A little bit," said Amelia Bedelia. "But you found me before I had the chance to get really creeped out."

"I would have been scared," said Alice.

"Finally is a true hero," said Pearl.

Alice sat straight up. "What was that?" she said.

"Was that some kind of animal?" asked Pearl.

"It sure was. We call him Jason," said Amelia Bedelia. "I forgot to tell you . . . my cousin snores. So loudly that we can hear him from the living room!"

Chapter 12

From Where to Here

The next morning before everyone headed back to town, Aunt Mary made an amazing breakfast, featuring blackberry pancakes, of course. Amelia Bedelia had volunteered to gather the blackberries by herself. She did it to get over her fear of falling. She had learned a long time ago that if you fall off your

bike, it's good to get right back on and ride again. Her parents made her promise not to pick berries anywhere near the money pit, of course.

CRACK

As she plucked the first berry, a *CRACK!* sounded right behind her. Amelia Bedelia whirled around. *BOOM!* She ran right into Jason, knocking them both to the ground. Jason was laughing.

"Got ya!" he said.

"You're mean," said Amelia Bedelia.

"It was just bubble gum," said Jason. "They sent me to make sure you don't fall into any more holes."

"That money pit should be an obstacle at Pirate Putt-Putt," said Amelia Bedelia.

"Amelia Bedelia, you were actually a hole in one," said Jason.

"Yo-ho-ho. Very funny," said Amelia Bedelia. "Where's my free eye patch?"

"How does it feel to be a golf ball?" said Jason.

"I'd rather be a goofball, like you," said Amelia Bedelia.

"Like me?" said Jason.

"Yes, I do," she said. "Thanks for making sure I was okay."

After that Amelia Bedelia and Alice settled in to summer at the shore. They sailed with Pearl, surfed with Jason and Roger, dug big holes in the sand with Finally,

read a lot of books and watched a lot of movies, and ate a ton of yummy summer beach food, especially ice cream and candy. The annual Beach Ball snuck up on everybody, just like it did every year.

"The town is starting to look like a pirate convention," said Amelia Bedelia's father, coming in from shopping for his costume. "You can't buy a lousy eye patch for twenty miles around."

Amelia Bedelia shrugged. "That's good. Who wants a lousy one?" she said.

Amelia Bedelia, Alice, and Jason weren't sure what they wanted to wear to the Beach Ball.

"I was able to dig up your costumes from last year," said Mary. "Maybe you can recycle something."

"Aunt Mary, please don't say dig up," said Amelia Bedelia.

"Sorry, I forgot," said Mary.

On the day of the Beach Ball, Amelia Bedelia, Alice, Pearl, and Jason arranged to meet near the *Whereami* on its float at the roundabout, where the parade would start. Pearl arrived carrying a small can of paint.

"What do you want me to touch up?" asked Pearl.

"Well, don't touch wet paint," said Amelia Bedelia. "You'll get it all over yourself. Use a brush."

The friends all climbed on the parade float with the ship, and Pearl pulled brushes out of her pocket.

"Perfect. Let's change some letters on the name *Whereami*," said Amelia Bedelia.

"Can you paint over the W and make the H into a capital letter?"

"That's all? That's easy," said Pearl, getting to work.

"Do you think we would have made good pirates?" asked Jason.

"Pirates were bad guys," said Amelia Bedelia.

"You can't be a good bad guy," said Alice.

"Being the best bad guy means you're the worst, right?" said Pearl.

"Bob's great . . . great . . . great-times-ten grandfather was probably a pirate," said Jason.

"That's okay. My favorite cousin was a pirate," said Amelia Bedelia.

"I am your *only* cousin," said Jason, laughing.

"Well, you're definitely a good guy," said Amelia Bedelia. "And so is Bob."

"Bob is a great guy," said Jason. "He's the best good guy there is."

"Yup," said Amelia Bedelia. Then she touched the piece of eight she had discovered on Blackberry Island. It was now hanging around her neck on a silver chain, a gift from Bob and Aunt Mary. "I can't wait to find out what he discovers about the history of that treasure."

The truck pulling the *Hereami* in the parade lurched ahead.

"Avast, mateys, we're under way!" said Jason.

"Jason, if they don't elect you mayor, come back and sack this town," said Alice.

"What kind of sack should he use? Paper or plastic?" said Amelia Bedelia.

"This is your dress rehearsal, Jason," said Alice. "For your campaign."

"Or shorts rehearsal," said Amelia Bedelia, pointing at Jason's board shorts and giggling.

"Look, there's your dad," said Jason.

Amelia Bedelia's father was crossing right in front of the truck pulling the *Hereami*. He was carrying four large milkshakes in a cardboard carrier. He must not have realized that the truck was moving. Slamming on his brakes, the truck driver let his air horn do the talking.

BAAAAAHHHHNNNNN!

Amelia Bedelia's father leaped into the air, sending the drinks flying.

"The driver of our ship just got your dad's attention," said Jason.

"Okay, see you guys later," said Pearl, climbing down from the ship while the truck driver helped Amelia Bedelia's father up.

"Aren't you going to ride with us?" said Amelia Bedelia.

"No, thanks. I've got my own boat," said Pearl. "Besides, I stashed a bunch of water balloons at the next intersection."

"What's the plan?" asked Alice. "Can I join you?"

"Absolutely!" said Pearl. "We'll meet you guys later."

"Thanks, Captain Pearl," said Jason, giving her a salute.

"You're welcome, Captain J," she said, saluting him back.

"We'll meet you for ice cream," said Amelia Bedelia, smiling.

She was happy that her best friends were such good friends with each other too.

As the parade continued and their ship passed by, spectators on both sides of the road burst into applause. Amelia Bedelia spotted her parents standing next to Bob and Aunt Mary. She waved to get their attention, then pointed at the new

name. Bob extended his spyglass to take a closer look. He laughed, giving them a thumbs-up.

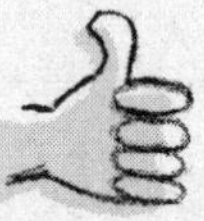

"Bob approves," said Jason.

He gave Amelia Bedelia a giant hug.

Sailing down Main Street on the good ship *Hereami*, Amelia Bedelia reached up to her necklace again, grasping the piece of eight. Rubbing it between her thumb and forefinger, she thought about all the people and moments in her life that had led her to this one right now. She couldn't help thinking about the ending of *Treasure Island*, when Long John Silver's parrot cries out, "Pieces of eight! Pieces of eight!" Amelia Bedelia kept rubbing her piece of eight, wishing that this voyage, and this summer, would never end.

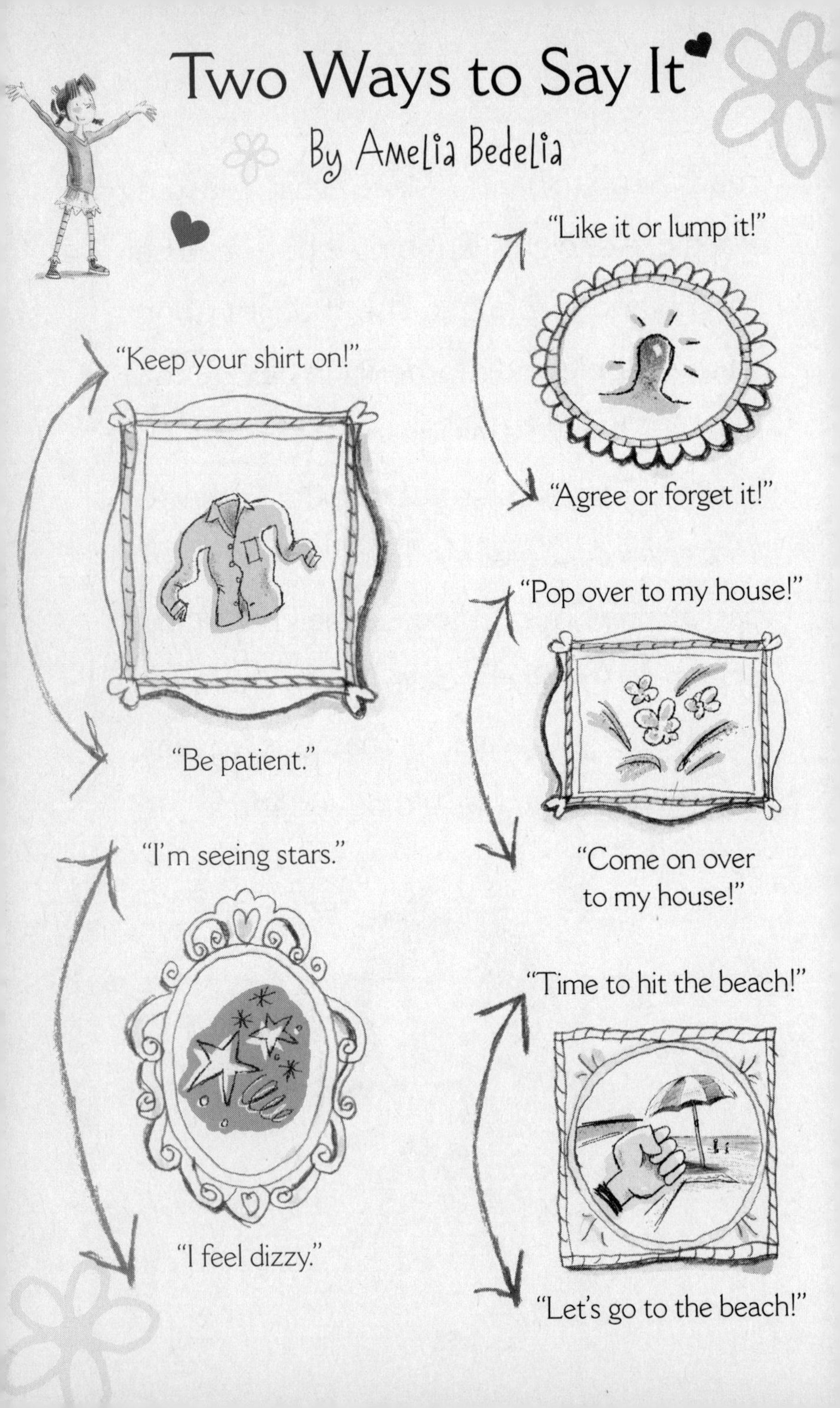
Two Ways to Say It
By Amelia Bedelia
"Keep your shirt on!"
"Be patient."
"I'm seeing stars."
"I feel dizzy."
"Like it or lump it!"
"Agree or forget it!"
"Pop over to my house!"
"Come on over to my house!"
"Time to hit the beach!"
"Let's go to the beach!"

"She tucked into her eggs."
"She ate her eggs."
"A labor of love."
"Something I really
want and like to do."
"This is my
stomping ground."
"This is where
I hang out."
"It's a money pit!"
"It just keeps costing
more and more."
"A hole in one!"
"A big success!"

Surf's Up with Amelia Bedelia

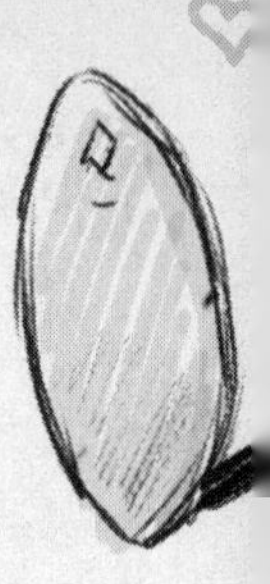

A short list of surfing terms

When you hit the crest of a wave and take off through the air.

Ankle Busters

These are super-small waves.

Axe

A huge wipeout.

Backwash

A wave that's heading back to the ocean; it sometimes hits new waves coming in.

Bail

When you think you going to crash or fall, you give up and let g of your surfboard.

Barrel

The barrel is the part of the wave inside the curl; it looks like a tube.

Beach Bum

A person who loves to hang out at the beach.

Burn

When you steal a wav that another surfer w about to ride.

When you make big, deep turns on the surface of the wave.

The very top part of the wave.

Dawn patro

Surfers who head t the beach early in t morning to surf!

When you push your board into and through a breaking wave.

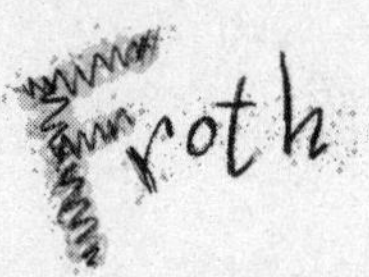

Being excited!

Gnarly

Very intense. Awesome!

Goofy Foot

Vhen you stand on
our board with your
ight foot forward.

Lip

The lip of the wave is the part at the top that curls over.

When you surf extremely well.

Vhen the wave
reaks and gets
frothy, that's
the soup.

When a wave curls over and a space is created inside it, that's the tube (also called a barrel).

The very bottom of the wave, the opposite of the crest.

With Amelia Bedelia anything can happen!

Have you read them all?

Amelia Bedelia wants a new bike—a brand-new shiny, beautiful, fast bike. A bike like that is really expensive and will cost an arm and a leg!

Amelia Bedelia is getting a puppy—a sweet, adorable, loyal, friendly puppy!

Amelia Bedelia is hitting the road. Where is she going? It's a surprise!

Amelia Bedelia is going to build a zoo in her backyard. Better yet, she is going to invite all her friends to bring their pets and help plan the exhibits and rides.

Amelia Bedelia usually loves recess, but one day she doesn't get picked for a team and she begins to have second thoughts about sports.

Amelia Bedelia and her friends are determined to find a cool clubhouse for their new club.

Amelia Bedelia is so excited to be spending her vacation at the beach! But one night, she sees her cousin sneaking out the window. Where is he going?

New steps inspire Amelia Bedelia and her dance school classmates to dance up a storm!

What does Amelia Bedelia want to be when she grows up? Turns out, the sky's the limit!

When disaster strikes and threatens to ruin her aunt's wedding, it's up to Amelia Bedelia to make sure Aunt Mary and Bob tie the knot!

An overnight camp is not Amelia Bedelia's idea of fun—especially not *this* camp, which sounds as though it's super boring and rustic. What Amelia Bedelia needs is a new plan, fast!